CLAUDE GUTMAN

# *the* EMPTY HOUSE

translated from the French by
ANTHEA BELL

PUFFIN BOOKS

### EDITORIAL NOTE

When the Nazis entered Paris in June 1940, the French government negotiated an armistice by which their country was divided into two zones. The north was to be governed by the anti-Semitic Nazis, which is why David has to leave Paris for Montreuil-sur-Mer under an assumed name. Later he travels by way of Paris into the southern zone, governed by Marshal Pétain from Vichy, which remained 'free' until 1943 when it, too, came under direct German occupation.

### PUFFIN BOOKS

Published by the Penguin Group
Penguin Books Ltd, 27 Wrights Lane, London W8 5TZ, England
Penguin Books USA Inc., 375 Hudson Street, New York, New York 10014, USA
Penguin Books Australia Ltd, Ringwood, Victoria, Australia
Penguin Books Canada Ltd, 10 Alcorn Avenue, Toronto, Ontario, Canada M4V 3B2
Penguin Books (NZ) Ltd, 182–190 Wairau Road, Auckland 10, New Zealand

Penguin Books Ltd, Registered Offices: Harmondsworth, Middlesex, England

First published by Editions Gallimard, Paris 1989
First published in Great Britain and Australia by Turton & Chambers 1991
Published in Puffin Books 1993
Reissued in Puffin Books 1995
1 3 5 7 9 10 8 6 4 2

Text copyright © Claude Gutman, 1989
English translation © Anthea Bell, 1991
All rights reserved

The moral right of the author has been asserted

Printed in England by Clays Ltd, St Ives plc
Set in Monotype Bembo

To all the murdered children in the world.

For Louba and Boris Pludermacher.

For my children, Colas, Olivier, Anne, who will carry the memory on.

To my adoptive town, Montreuil-sous-Bois.

Events on the grand scale, mass sufferings, catch the imagination and arouse compassion only incompletely and in an abstract way. We need a specific example to arouse our love or fear. We are so made that the face of a weeping child touches us more than hearing that a whole province has died of starvation.

Joseph Kessel

EVERY evening without exception, despite my glum face, I would tuck my pyjamas under my arm. Then I climbed two flights of stairs and knocked six times at the Bianchottis' door, as agreed. They would open it, smiling, hug me, and lead me to their son's room. No more smiles as Madame Bianchotti turned the door handle. This room was sacred, preserved exactly as it had been on the day he left. Because he never came back. Two policemen brought a letter saying he had 'died for France'. There was a citation and a handsome medal as well. The Bianchottis had never got over it. They wept for days on end. Madame Bianchotti had rushed down two flights of stairs to throw herself into Mother's arms, and never mind the sewing machine or the hem which was going to need restitching.

She flung herself on Mother, wailing, 'He was so young! So very young! Oh, say it can't be true, Madame Grunbaum. Say he'll come back.'

She began crying again, and so did Mother, holding Madame Bianchotti in her arms. I cried myself, and I could see Father felt like it too. But he dried his tears and left his cutting-out table to come and comfort Madame Bianchotti. Nothing he could say was any good, she was wailing so loudly. So he just put his hand on Madame Bianchotti's shoulder, pressing it hard. In Yiddish, he asked Mother to make a cup of tea; perhaps that might calm her. Then he turned to me.

'War's a foul thing, David,' he said. 'War's a foul, filthy thing.'

And he went back to his cutting-out table.

Madame Bianchotti never did dry her tears; she took them with her along with her shopping bag all round the neighbourhood, into the queues outside the empty shops. Monsieur Bianchotti did not weep or wail again. He just fell silent, and stayed that way. He never went out any more. He spent his waking hours looking at his son's framed photograph on the mantelpiece of the room into which I went every evening without exception, my pyjamas tucked under my arm.

Once I used to sleep at home in the normal way, in my own bed. Mother kissed me goodnight, Father kissed me goodnight. And I lay in the dark thinking of anything I liked. Good marks or bad marks at school, thumping Dugrant for sneaking on Rebérioux and saying he had cheated in class. It was *my* bed. *My* room. *My* books. *My* bedside light. Then, suddenly, I lost it all, and I had to go and sleep in a dead man's room. Madame Bianchotti had changed nothing in it except to add a folding bed for me. It squealed as it unfolded, and went on squealing while I lay there with my eyes wide open, just in case the dead man unexpectedly came back to claim his room. It took me a long time to get to sleep, and then I slept badly. Even though Madame Bianchotti had made sacrifices for me, giving me a mouse hole in that museum of hers. She polished the floor twice a week. I always put slippers on before I went in. I'd have liked to slide on the floor, but the little table, the lace coverlet and the crucifix hanging over the bed so terrified me that I never even sketched a dance step. I mustn't move, or the ghost might notice I was there. I must try not to breathe. My mind just kept on going round and round and round until I was worn out. I lay thinking perhaps the dead man wasn't dead after all, or I reran newsreels in my head, the cinema newsreels showing air raids at the time when the Maginot line was supposed to be impregnable. If he was really dead then I liked to think of him with two red holes in his right side, an idea I got from a poem we'd learnt by heart at school, when the poet Rimbaud goes for a walk in the country. I could imagine Bertrand Bianchotti better like that. He often used to play with me when I was little and I met him on the stairs, carrying a bucket to be emptied down the lavatory between the floors of our block of flats. He wanted to be a motor mechanic. He had begun his apprenticeship, and then he ended up 'dying for France'. With a nice citation. Apparently he trod on a mine. But however he actually died, I wasn't going to see him again, and neither were his mother or father, and his citation would never be any use for anything.

That was all way back in the past.

I got a medal too, like the rest of the family. A star-shaped medal made of yellow cloth. You had to wear it sewn to your left lapel. It was black-edged, and the word JEW was black too, so as to show up better. Mother had sewn it on with her best thread. That way we kept in line.

'You have to keep in line,' said Father. 'France is the land of liberty, and if you keep in line there's nothing to fear. French law has always protected Jews – well, except for Captain Dreyfus, maybe, but that was just one historic mistake. And anyway they put it right later. So you have to keep in line.'

Father's eyes, sparkling with mischief. Father's wreath of hair. I liked it when he spoke French with his foreign accent, or when he read the newspaper, running his finger along the lines and turning to me for help when he had trouble with a word.

'It's my glasses again, they don't focus properly. Have a look at this, David.'

You were so proud of being French, and knowing that your wife was French and your son would never go through your own horrible experiences. To be French was profoundly important to you.

You sometimes took our naturalization deed out of the dining-room drawer and kissed it like a good-luck charm. Just three names written on an official sheet of paper. You used to show it to Mother. You used to show it to me.

'French, David, remember you're French!' you said.

And then I'd look at you and be glad to see your eyes shine with a childlike happiness, briefly banishing the sorrow there inside you ever since . . .

That's another story, and I think I'll tell it at this point.

'The Poles are anti-Semites, David,' Father told me. 'Dogs, savages, filth, the lot of them. You have to know that. The whole world has to know that.'

'Oh, do leave him alone,' said Mother. 'You can see he's too young for such things.'

But I was sitting on Father's knee, and he was telling me a story. My very own 'Little Red Riding Hood', except that there wasn't any huntsman at the end to cut the big bad wolf open and let the little girl and her grandmother out. No happy ending. It was a story to make you cry and give you nightmares.

'You have to know these things. The Poles –' And Father's voice broke. But he told me his story.

'I'm old to be your father, David. It's better to have young parents. But you're the only child I have left. All of the others –'

His voice became inaudible, but I knew the whole story by heart. He looked at me. He hugged me tight. He looked at Mother with such love that it made the story he had to tell even more terrible.

Once upon a time, in a place far, far away in the atlas with its coloured maps, somewhere near the Soviet Union, there was a remote little village, almost cut off from the world. Now and then a pedlar passed by, bringing news from the nearby villages and the big city. He sold newspapers too, so the whole village could catch up with what was going on in the outside world, though rather a long time after it had happened. Not that the news was much use to them. The villagers lived plainly. They were poor, they would always be poor, they could only dream of the big ship which would take them to America some time, America where even the poorest of the poor could get rich in a single day.

America! What a place! But Father didn't care about America. He was a tailor, setting his sewing machine up out of doors. There was a photograph of him with his wife Rachel and his three children. Because that was the point of the story. I was Father's fourth child, and Mother was his second wife. He often talked about his other children and his first wife when he had nightmares. He howled their names. 'Isaac, Elias, Sarah!' My unknown brothers and sister. And he cried, 'Rachel, Rachel! No, no, stop, don't do it, don't!' Then he would wake, sitting up in bed, sweating, exhausted, distraught, with Mother soothing him like a child.

'It was only a bad dream, Jacob.'

But all three of us knew his nightmare had really happened. One day, unexpectedly, a gang of anti-Semitic Poles came to the village by night, and no prayers of the rabbi's could stop them. They were drunk, armed with axes, swords, knives and hunting rifles, and they had invaded the houses by the light of the torches they carried. First they set fire to the synagogue, and when people ran out to extinguish the flames they began cutting them down, shouting 'Jewish dogs!' Then they broke down the doors of the houses. No one could stop them in their rampage.

'Hush, Jacob, you know this is no kind of story for a child his age!'

'He *must* know. He *must*. He must know, for his children's sake. So that he can tell them, and it will never happen again. He must tell them, you see.'

Mother knew he was right, and she went away, leaving us to our story, which was always the same, never a word changed. A picture from a history book, with Father in the foreground, in front of the flames and smoke rising from the burning synagogue. The Poles broke down his door with an axe, and in cold blood, before Father's eyes, they strangled his wife Rachel and his children Isaac, Elias and Sarah. They left Father himself for dead on the mud floor of the living room.

They killed children like me, whose only crime was to have been born Jews, just for being Jews.

I've seen my father cry. And I saw he was not ashamed of his tears, although he was a grown man. I sat on his knee, a little boy who couldn't comfort his father. How can you comfort a person for something like that? I cried too, as we hugged each other, each in his own way imagining that scene, which lasted only a few minutes, ending with blood drying on the dusty floor where the three murdered children and my father's first wife Rachel lay.

Mother picked me out of Father's arms, hugged me, and I clung to her. Father had dried his tears, and could go on.

'When I came round, my head was bleeding, but I was alive. Alive, you hear? Fifty Jews died that night. Five hundred escaped. Why me? I ask you, why me? If you'd heard the wailing in the village, if you'd seen the wrecked houses, I'm sure you would have done as I did,' he said.

'Of course. I'd have helped you.'

He had looked at his dead wife and children. He kissed them, smearing them with his own blood. Then he lifted up his voice and howled, cursing God. Wild howls, while the village lay desolate now that the screaming had stopped. He cursed a foul God who could not protect his own people, a vile God who would let such dearly loved beings die like dogs, who allowed the executioners to do their work generation after generation. A God who could never be trusted again. The rabbi tried to reason with Father and told him this was sent by the Almighty to try him. By way of reply Father punched his nose. Then he left the village with nothing at all, walking the roads alone, a few photographs next to his heart, his body full of tears, his sewing machine over his shoulder.

'Yes, I ran away, and I know I'm not a coward. But what else could I have done? Stayed in my house, weeping? No, David, life is always stronger than death. I know that now. It's always stronger. And your mother is the proof of it!'

Her loving glance at Father showed me that all right. Nothing but a glance. A loving glance.

And then the story went on, like 'The Brave Little Tailor', with lots more episodes. Father told me how he came to France. I heard a little more of the story every evening. About the crooks in Danzig who took his savings, promising to stow him away on a freighter bound for Argentina. Father gave them the money. The stowaways were to assemble in secret on the quayside that evening. They got into an old tub which cast off, went once round the harbour and came back to shore. A dozen of the crooks, armed with sticks, fell on the credulous passengers, shouting, 'Quick, quick, the police – they've spotted us!'

And there they all were, back on the quayside, with their small children crying and the thieves gone. So much for Argentina.

Father sold his sewing machine to cross the German border. He worked in a coal mine. He had remembered everything. He only knew that France stood at the end of the road. He earned enough to keep from starving. Then the mine closed. Men were laid off. There were strikes. Father saw the Germans starving too, while Yantel, a Jew like himself, made speeches to the miners. 'Workers of the world, unite!' But Father himself was a Socialist, not a Communist. He used to read the journal of the *Bund*, the Jewish Socialist organization, back in that place he did not like to think of any more. He had a row with Yantel, and the pair of them ended up getting arrested by the German police and expelled over the border into Belgium. They laughed, Yantel and Father did. They laughed because they could still laugh. They roared with laughter, because they were Jewish, and one might be Communist and the other Socialist, but never mind the insults they hurled at each other, they faced the Belgian police with a sense of firm friendship and nothing else in the world.

Their laughter rang in my head as I lay in bed, thinking of the part of his story Father had told that evening. I wanted tomorrow to come quickly.

Tomorrow came. And there sat Father on my bed, laughing again. He rose and stepped back so that I could see him better, standing there in the middle of *my* room. Suddenly he began fooling about, hopping on one leg, staggering, and still roaring with laughter.

'That's the way I earned my living in Brussels, David. Yantel and I. The two of us posing naked in front of a bunch of art students, trying not to lose our balance. Yantel and I dared not look at each other, or we'd have been hysterical with laughter. I was supposed to be a javelin thrower at the end of his run, and Yantel was a mountain shepherd. All the students laughed while their teacher yelled at us. "Don't wobble! Keep your balance, you fools, can't you!" So we got the sack, and ended up still laughing in a café over a beer. A good beer it was, too.'

That was the only time Father seemed to forget the rest of it. But I still had pictures of flames and murder going through my head.

Then to France, in secret. Always in secret, as if Father were forbidden to live in the daylight. Just one tiny border to be crossed by night, unobtrusively. Hiding, always hiding. And then Paris, the capital of liberty.

'Never forget you owe everything to France, David.'

Father looked at Mother yet again. As if she had been there when he arrived, waiting to pick him up just before he collapsed. As if he had taken refuge in her arms, escaping the round-ups staged by the police when they cordoned off a whole lot of people and checked their papers.

Loving, soft, warm Mother. But I don't have time to write about Mother now. She's not here any more. Father's not here any more. I miss them. I have to live without them.

'You must live, David, whatever happens you must live,' Father said.

And it was to make sure I lived that Father gave

me that slap in the face, one evening after dinner.

I was standing up to him. 'I won't go and sleep at the Bianchottis'! I've got a perfectly good room of my own.'

'We are not going to have an argument about this, David. This evening, and every evening after this, you will sleep at the Bianchottis'.'

I looked imploringly at Mother. She obviously agreed with Father. I started shouting.

'I won't! I won't, I won't!'

For the first time in my life I saw Father go absolutely white, and his hand shot out like lightning and slapped my face. A slap given out of love. I didn't realize until later, much later. Not until now.

Mother tried to comfort me. I pushed her away. Father tried to say goodnight. I turned my back on him. I went to my room, got my pyjamas, climbed two floors up and entered the dead man's room for the first time.

I didn't sleep well.

Why, I wondered, why that unexplained slap? Why the hatred in his face? Why did Mother back him up? Everyone was against me. They ought to have told me. They ought to have explained, as they did before, instead of leaving me in the dark. Or talking to each other very fast in Yiddish, hoping I wouldn't understand. When I was little I used to tell my school friends my parents spoke fluent English, with a perfect accent. There were three of us the same in my class at school, Hirsh, Kerbel and me. And to us it might as well have been English. But only Grunbaum — that was me — really learnt to understand and speak it. Everyone was sure I would be an interpreter later. However, before I could understand my father's slap I had to interpret it for myself, in my own language of French. Perfect French, with the upstrokes and downstrokes wet with tears. Why were they sending me away, when this was my home?

When I came downstairs next morning, pink-eyed like a white rabbit, Mother was waiting for me. From the look of her, I could tell her thoughts had been as gloomy as my own. Father's drawn face told the same story. So why the silence? Didn't I have a right to know, at my age?

Father got his word in even before Mother flung her arms round me to comfort me.

'Now listen, David, from today you have to do as I say and ask no questions. For your own good. It's a matter of life or death. This is serious, very serious. I can't say any more than that. I never ought to have hit you, but it was for your own good, understand?'

Well, I understand now, but I didn't before. You were right, perfectly right, but if only you knew how I felt! How I wanted to punch you in the face, wished I was strong enough to floor you with a single blow. I was only thirteen, though, unable to do anything but dream of getting my own back, and I swear I did dream of it all through my sleepless night. My own good? What did you know about it? You did your best, I know. You did all you could to stop me turning out like you, to keep me from poverty and unhappiness. Thank you. But I had forgotten it that night.

I forgot all the times you left your cutting-out table or your thimble to come and bend over my exercise book, watching me carefully writing big Es and the twiddly decorative bits of big Bs. I forgot how your own tongue stuck out slightly like mine. You got me to recite the things I'd learnt by heart: dates from history, stuff from ethics lessons and natural history lessons, and then you ran your hand through my hair.

'You'll go far, my boy.'

I knew that in the evenings, after ten hours' work in your shop two buildings away from the flat, you secretly opened my satchel, and with Mother's help you tried to learn the things I had mastered so quickly. You wanted to be able to understand more than what you read in the Yiddish journal *Unzer Schtime*, 'Our Voice', the gospel of the *Bund*. You had learnt to read and write French, of course, but you still didn't speak it perfectly, getting vowels mixed up, making a real mess of it.

I forgot the overtime you worked making clothes to measure, the subcontracted orders you took on so that you could pay for piano lessons from the old lady with the hairy chin.

'Rubinstein! You'll be better than Rubinstein, I swear you will!'

Personally, I wanted to be a racing cyclist. I practised my scales, but pedals put me in mind of the Tour de France cycle race more than Bach and Chopin.

The piano came for Christmas when I was nine. The most wonderful and expensive present that my parents could give me. Clearly I was going to be famous.

I can see you both now, watching me play it. You put your hand on Mother's shoulder, Father. Reserved as you usually were, you allowed yourself that rare, clumsy gesture. Father, Mother, how you both blushed when I looked at you! And you quickly took your hand away, Father. The sound of Clementi's sonatinas hung in the air. I flung myself into your arms in front of the Christmas tree. Because we had a Christmas tree.

'It's silly, really, David,' Father told me. 'But you have to go along with the custom of the country.'

He said so every year, and told me about another, unfamiliar festival. But I'm sure that when he gave me my presents he must have thought of the others, the family he had left behind, who used to celebrate something mysterious called Hanukkah around the same time of year, in winter. He named it with much feeling.

'Hanukkah lasted a week, David. The first evening you lit two candles on the big candlestick, and then one a day all through the week, and at the end of the week you had a party.'

He said no more. All those past Hanukkahs were

going through his head, and perhaps the presents he had given my dead brothers and sister too. Poor people's presents, but given with love. I don't know what they were like, but I could guess they were nice presents from the way Father's eyes shone with tears. And perhaps they had a special, festive meal, with beans or chicken? I shall never know.

I was king of a Christian festival. We even listened to Midnight Mass on the wireless. And then came the black, shiny lacquered piano. I started playing sonatinas again, to please my parents, playing with love this time. With a love as deep as the ocean Father once wanted to cross. The same love I feel for you now. But I can only write it down on the squared paper of this exercise book. You've gone. You're not here any more. My words will never reach you again. Your voices will never speak to me any more. Or perhaps I'm wrong, perhaps they will . . .

I've been missing you so long, ever since that dreadful day. It was so dreadful I don't want to write about it. But it's always there, Father. Just as the day that gang of thugs came to destroy your remote little village was always there for you.

Who would have thought it? France had given you its hospitality, a wife, a son, a tailor's shop in the inner suburbs of Paris. Quarter of an hour's walk from the Porte de Montreuil, beyond the places where I was forbidden to go. A shop with your name up over it, in the Rue Garibaldi, almost on the corner of the Rue de la Révolution. It seemed a good omen.

Yantel and his wife visited us every Saturday evening. Mother used to smile, looking at me. I knew. In the middle of the meal you two would start in on the conversation you had begun years before in Germany, which never reached a conclusion. It was full of bawling. Shouting. Laughter, Coffee. Stalin. Communism. Socialism. How to make the world a better place. Hitler. They knew it practically off by heart. Mother and Madame Yantel used to take refuge in the kitchen. I stayed there open-mouthed, listening. You talked so loud, you must both have been right.

'There's going to be war, Jacob, and only the Soviet Union can help us.'

'War, war – you're always on about war! Ever heard of peace?'

Yantel stuck to his point. 'Jacob, we can none of us do anything on our own. We have to join together. You know they're arresting Communists and Jews in Germany?'

'I know, I know, and Communist Jews are worse off than anyone. You said all that before, last week. But what do you think we have to fear in France? Anti-Semites? You get them everywhere. But you won't change the world, Yantel. Did your Communist friends succeed, in Spain?'

'And did your Socialist Zionist friends succeed in Israel?'

It was like a boxing match. I understood nothing except that it was about some Jewish war, like the games of cowboys and Indians we played at school. Or no, not really, because we were playing for fun, and they were serious. Or then again, perhaps not all that serious, because they would suddenly look at each other and start chuckling, laughing, swapping memories, and their words escaped me. Having exchanged insults, they were friends again. Friends, and French.

'Now then, David, let's hear you play that piano.'

I played for them, played my best, played as well as I possibly could. The word peace meant something important. But Chopin had been Polish. Was he anti-Semitic?

Anti-Semitic is a word I must have heard over and over again, without taking much notice of it. It just kept cropping up, like a tune which didn't interest me. Nobody seemed anti-Semitic in our little neighbourhood between the Rue Garibaldi, the Rue de la Révolution, the Rue de Paris and the Rue Marceau.

Madame Ducamp sometimes gave me sweets when I went to fetch the bread – I was to ask for a loaf 'not too brown on top' – and Monsieur Armellino let me come into his cabinet-maker's workshop where he stood ankle-deep in wood shavings. I could have stayed there for hours. Father had made him a Sunday suit which really fitted. He was only one metre forty-five tall.

'More customers like him and you'd save plenty

on cloth,' Mother said, smiling.

They mentioned, over supper, being sorry for him because he was so short and he had no wife. Perhaps that's why he looked so unhappy. In his place I'd have married one of the female dwarfs from the circus which came once a year to perform at the Porte de Montreuil. Poor Monsieur Armellino! He never stopped working. Even at night you could see the light in his workshop window.

So who was anti-Semitic? Not the schoolteachers; Father would have sworn to that. I was the only one out of my whole class at the Robespierre Primary School to pass the exam into grammar school. The only one.

'That's what living in France means,' Father said on that occasion, raising his champagne glass, pouring Yantel some more, and hugging me tight. 'I'm proud of you, David! To see your name there on the list!'

And he ran his hand through my hair. Mother closed her eyes to avoid seeing her little boy – getting quite big now – drink wine. Horror of horrors! But this was a special day. Not only was I going to be as good at the piano as Rubinstein, I might even, heaven help me, get to be Prime Minister, like Léon Blum, or I might be a famous doctor, a consultant with a brass plate outside my door. Or then again, I might be . . .

However, I hardly had time for any of that.

Mother and Father were listening to the wireless

all day long, because Yantel's predictions had come true, and there was a war on.

For a long time nothing at all happened. And then suddenly a lot happened, fast. In a very short time.

'The newspapers are lying,' Father said firmly.

I believed him. But when the Germans entered Paris, I actually saw them.

'No,' said Father. 'No, I will never leave my home and my shop. Never! What do you think they can do to us? I've done enough running in my life. I'm tired of it. Yantel can go if he wants to – I'm staying here in Montreuil.'

'Then let's send David to the country.'

'Certainly not!' And Father started shouting. 'He's staying here with us. I tell you, there's no risk. The wireless and the newspapers are lying. They won't do anything. I shall just go on working. I'm not afraid.'

There was such certainty in his voice.

In fact Mother and Father didn't do much working. Or rather, they did, but not on the sewing machine or with needle and thread. They even enlisted me, after school hours, to help the cowards who wanted to run away – because they were all cowards to Father, and that was all there was to it. As the Germans approached with the aim, so rumour said, of razing Paris to the ground, solidarity still meant something to him. These people were cowards, yes, but first and foremost they were human beings. So Father was here, there and everywhere, helping our neighbours to get well away from Paris. Those who hadn't already gone earlier, when trains were still running.

I couldn't make it out. We were staying. So what about all those stories of massacres Father had told me? And the pictures that scared me on Pathé News at the cinema, before the big film began? If I'd been him, I'd have gone. The ogres were coming. Real ogres, not like the ogres in 'Tom Thumb', and they were bad enough and made me feel scared. But these were real-life ogres with cannon that had great gaping mouths. However, they didn't scare Father, or Monsieur Armellino on the other side of the road. He too quietly lent a hand with the straps of suitcases, which were loaded up on handcarts from goodness knows where, even on babies' prams, and set off for nowhere in particular.

While Mother and Father helped the neighbours from the various floors of the building to pack anything and everything, without much regard for their linen cupboards and store cupboards, and comforted Madame Dugrand, who was sure she'd never make it, with her walking stick, they left me in charge of the shop.

All the neighbours came to the shop, because they knew we were staying. And all those people smiled nicely at me, whether they were friends of mine or not. They slipped me money, gave me their latchkeys – 'and please ask your parents to keep an eye open for burglars.' Personally, I thought the burglars would have cleared out themselves by now and be well on their way to the Loire, to burgle whatever they could find there. There was a war on, and I made a packet in tips, but not a word to Mother and Father about that.

Within a week the shop was like Ali Baba's cave.

'See how they trust us, David!' said Father.

Such pride! He was a naturalized refugee, not a native Frenchman, and here were all these French people trusting him with their worldly goods.

'There's stuff worth millions in the shop, David, millions! And I shall see they get every bit of it back safe.'

Mother could hardly make her way through to her sewing machine, but what would she have sewn? People had left their clothes behind, taking only essentials with them in their haste. I saw them leave with those essentials – things that would never be the slightest use to them: an old clock in need of repair, an old picture of a hunting scene with deer in the undergrowth, the complete works of Shakespeare in six volumes – but they valued them so highly. That's what makes something essential: it has no practical use, but it does your heart good. Or not, as the case may be. I know. I've had experience of that. Anyway, they left the rest in our shop: a Louis Something-or-other chest of drawers, piles of sheets, high-backed armchairs of the kind called Voltaire chairs, like the name of my grammar school. A sort of museum annexe, with everything labelled ready for the day when it would all be given back.

And to think I laughed unfeelingly to see that

what they thought would be really useful was a framed photograph of an old grandpa with a moustache, surrounded by his family on the day of the eldest son's wedding. What earthly use could that be to them in the crush on the roads which began at the corner of our street? The traffic jams of Montreuil: wheelbarrows, cars and pedal carts.

We stayed behind. So did the ogres. In fact they settled in very fast, in a midsummer desert with all the shutters closed. I went on playing the piano with the windows open while Mother and Father looked after the stuff people had left with them. I wanted to see the Germans. I had been so scared of their arrival, but nothing had happened to me yet. I went as far as the Rue d'Avron on my bike, and saw them marching up and down the streets in uniform. I turned and cycled back fast, very fast, to warn Mother and Father. To my disappointment they had seen some Germans before I did, in the Rue de Paris, on their way back to the Croix de Chavaux in armoured cars.

Alone against *them*. With only a few people in the streets, almost all the shops closed, and Father, who insisted on believing the information broadcast from the German cars, with their loudspeakers. 'Keep calm,' they said. 'You are in no danger.'

I was alone. All my school friends had left. I went across the street to see Monsieur Armellino, who had not gone either.

'Don't you worry, David, they'll be gone again as fast as they came,' he said. 'Once our lot really get to work – well, you wait and see!'

He talked like Yantel, although he never said the word Jew. In fact he didn't say anything much, but I could hear the hatred in his quiet voice. He went on planing wood, on and on without stopping. There was such strength in that little man – and to think I used to laugh at him.

I wonder where Monsieur Armellino is now? He used to read a Socialist newspaper, I understood. I hope he's alive, I hope I'll see him again some day. I hope he's out there in the Resistance with a rifle, a pistol, anything, picking them off like rabbits. I wish Monsieur Armellino knew. I trust him. Would he help me find Mother and Father? I expect he's leading a Resistance group somewhere. He'll find them for me. I'm sure he's a leader, he's in charge, he'll know what to do. He stayed behind when the Germans took over in Paris. And I'm sure that when he talked to me that day, he knew what he was going to do. Because a little later he left, just shut up his cabinet-maker's shop and went off without a word to anyone. Sometimes I searched the lists put up on the walls for his name, to see if the Germans were after him and wanted to shoot him. But I guess he'd have done them some damage first, a lot of damage, and then he'd have managed to escape.

Oh, the hell with all the little details in this story. The hell with Monsieur Armellino being only one metre forty-five tall. The hell with the colour of German uniforms. The hell with what Father said.

'If one of them dares show his face here, I'll kill him with my hands, or with this,' he said, and he went to find a hatchet he had hidden under a roll of cloth. He was sure that would protect us, Mother and me.

The hell with it. The hell with everything. I wish I could smash everything to bits. Blow it all up. Get my revenge, kill and kill and kill . . .

I've been holding this pencil so tight my fingers hurt. I'd like to strangle those murderers. I can't bear it. I'm going to cry.


I had to leave this exercise book for a bit. I've come back to it now. I went for a walk in the countryside. Then I ran. I got breathless, shouting and kicking trees and clods of earth. But I have to come and sit down again and write, tell the whole story even if I don't want to, even if my throat is swollen with hatred and tears and my hand trembles. I have to do what Father wants. Or does he still want?

'When he's grown up, and finished his studies, he'll tell the story of what we went through, so that it can never happen again.' That's what he said. 'Yes, he'll tell the story.'

Words which come back to me as if from millions of light years away. Very close, really. But that's not exactly what Father meant.

He wanted it all told, every little bit, even the smallest details. I understood after I'd been out just now. Father, Mother, say I'll see you again! You'll be proud of me. *I'm* the one who wants to tell the whole story now.

How pleased we all were after that horrible, bleak summer when the armistice was signed, and the people who had gone away came back. You could hardly hide your pleasure in being proved right, Father. Nothing too bad had happened.

They came back looking slightly embarrassed, there were copious thanks, and the hugging was even more enthusiastic when Yantel came into the shop just as you were returning the keys of his flat to Monsieur Luquet, the cheesemonger from the Rue de la Révolution, and he was offering you the pick of his cheeses whenever you liked, 'and a thousand thanks'.

You and Yantel embraced like two brothers who had parted centuries ago. Only three months – but a solid five minutes of hugging. Not a word spoken, just the way you looked at one another, holding each other close as you both wept, hiding the tears for the sake of your dignity. Mother held me close, too. She shared your happiness. There were others who had not been so lucky, and would never come back for their labelled belongings.

We realized when Yantel told us about the hot sun, the weariness, the lack of water, cars breaking down, the country people watching the crowd go by, the looters, the army deserters, and then, suddenly, Italian aircraft nose-diving to attack, raking the road with machine-gun fire.

Mother and Father listened attentively, and I drank in Yantel's words. He told us about lost, crying children who might or might not be taken in. He told us about the scribbled messages stuck up on telegraph poles or the notice boards outside village halls. Y seeks Z: meet at F. He told us about the crossing of the Loire just as the Germans blew up the bridges. He told us about the dead left unburied who rotted in the sun, about ladies in white gloves and high-heeled shoes weeping over their blisters and the jewels they had had to give in exchange for a bit of bread or ham. He told us everything.

I had settled myself without his noticing.

'Nobody wanted to fight, Jacob. Nobody. I saw soldiers putting on dead men's clothes so as to look like civilians. It's a funny thing, Jacob, I wasn't even horrified. I just felt a deep distaste. And well, when it comes to walking, I feel the same as you. We've done about enough of it.'

This was really war. It had spared us, though.

Yantel asked about the members of the Friendly Association, and what had become of them.

The Friendly Association was a group Father had belonged to which met on Wednesdays. A group of friends, hence the name: Jewish friends who lived in Montreuil. The Israelite Friendly Association of Montreuil was its full name, and you could hardly wish for better friends, although Father would call them terrible names on Thursdays.

( 33 )

'That hypocrite so-and-so! That Communist what's-his-name! That fool of a thingummy!'

It was as if insults and rude remarks were all the French Father had really mastered, although he stopped as soon as he saw the end of my little Jewish nose pointing in his direction. I had learnt about the shape of my nose, you see. It had started appearing in all the papers. If you're Jewish you have a hooked nose, ears that stick out, hair in ringlets and fingers with curved, witch-like nails at the end. This was not quite what I saw in my mirror. I saw a perfectly straight nose, and quite neatly shaped ears. As for the long, curving nails, I didn't think anyone in the Association had those. But there wasn't any Association now. It had gone. So I had no way of making sure.

'The Jablonskis are back. So are the Rosinskis.'

Father had told Yantel the names of everyone who was around. The others had vanished, leaving no address.

'They'll have gone into hiding in the country, Jacob.'

'Gone into hiding? What for? Have I gone into hiding?'

'Oh, for heaven's sake, stop being such a damn fool, Jacob!'

Yantel had started shouting. He had called Father a fool. I wasn't standing for that. I got to my feet, and I punched him hard on his nose. His Jewish nose, the Jewish nose out of the newspaper. Yantel's nose started streaming with blood.

'You've got no right to say that, Yantel. You've got no right to call Father a fool – you're the fool, you're the one who ran away and now you're preaching sermons! It's horrible, that's what it is, Yantel, and you're horrible, and I hate you!'

And I ran to my room and locked myself in.

Yantel was still around at supper-time, though there wasn't much to eat. He looked at me with his fine, piercing blue eyes.

'I apologize for what I said, David,' he told me.

And strange to say, he and Father went on talking, with no more rude remarks about each other. But I wasn't listening. I had made Yantel back down. I had avenged Father. Getting an apology was what mattered. I'd humiliated Yantel, and he was apologizing. He was braver than me. Words can hurt more than fists.

Father, I love you so much. Mother, I love you so much. It's hard to put it into words. Yantel was right. Perhaps that's why you're not here any more. Yantel said we had to fight, or if fighting was impossible, to run. Personally, he said, he was going to fight, even with his bare hands, until the Nazis went. You were so sure it would be all right that you didn't listen to him, Father, because you were doing as the authorities said, so it was all in order.

So when the first summons came you didn't hesitate for a moment.

We all three went on foot to the Croix de

Chavaux police station. I walked beside you and Mother; both of you were in your Sunday best, walking proudly, slowly, enjoying an hour off. Just going for a walk, having taken those precious papers they wanted out of the dining-room drawer: the deed of naturalization and our identity cards, wrapped in beautiful, soft tissue paper.

The law was the law. You had to obey it. And what harm was there in that? It was all in order.

On our way down the Rue de Paris – it was early autumn and a nice day for a walk – you took me by the shoulder, Father.

'If you'd been a girl we were going to call you France. Nice name, don't you think, France?' you said.

Shameful France. France full of little busybody officials just doing their job, blindly applying the rules. France, horrible France! That was the France I saw when we got to the police station, with bicycles standing in its little yard. There was already a crowd, and Father realized we were in for a long afternoon. He knew some of the people in the queue. They included all those members of the Association who had come back to Montreuil. There were friendly greetings. I'd grown, but people were still patting me on the head. They'd held me on their knees when I was tiny. 'Remember, Jacob?' Father remembered. In fact we were going against German regulations in that tiny yard. They'd forbidden all public gatherings. They said so on the wireless.

'Our revenge,' said Monsieur Rosenbaum.

Everyone laughed. Then, as they waited for their turn, they started talking Yiddish, and their voices rose, telling old stories I didn't understand. They were laughing. But silence fell when the first in the queue came back again, trembling, looking grim.

Wordlessly they showed their identity cards, stamped with the word JEW in capital letters. They went away.

'Here it comes,' someone said. 'Why not stamp us on the forehead? That'd be easier to spot from a distance.'

There was anger in his voice.

Father didn't flinch. He squeezed my hand very tight.

Nobody knew the man who had spoken. He looked at us all.

'I will never accept this shame,' he said. He was almost incoherent. Then he walked away.

Only now did I realize that there were lots of Jews who weren't really Jews: they didn't look Jewish, or belong to the Association. Jews who had emerged from nowhere. Jews you'd never have believed were Jews. Father was staggered. He pointed to someone in the little crowd – it's not polite to point, but he couldn't help himself, and he wanted to show me. He had spotted Madame Laclos the florist, who was always visiting the nuns in the convent near the French Radio building and the Place de la République. He had been sure she was anti-Semitic. Nobody could make it out. The real Jews, the ones who didn't hide it, suddenly discovered that there were other Jews, underground Jews, who might as well have come from another planet.

I didn't understand about that until later, when Madame Lonia explained the war to us, spreading some documents out in front of her.

'People classified as Jewish are those who belong or who have belonged to the Jewish religion, or who have more than two Jewish grandparents (grandfathers or grandmothers). Grandparents who belong or have belonged to the Jewish religion are considered to be Jews. Jews who have fled from the occupied zone are forbidden to return there.'

Lonia read out the date of the decree – it was 27 September 1940. She read it out loud, in the room where I'm writing now. She drew arrows on the blackboard. I knew what she meant about the zones, because I'd been around a good deal by then.

Our turn to go into the police station. The policeman sitting at a desk entered our names in a large book, in alphabetical order. Then he took his stamp and marked all those precious papers, the deed of naturalization, and our identity cards with the word JEW.

He did his stamping automatically, without any pleasure in his work. His bosses had told him to do it, so he did.

Father was white when he came out, clinging to Mother's arm. Then he took a deep breath of air.

'There, you see, nothing happened! It's all in

order now. Come on, let's go home.'

Mother and Father went back to work in the shop. But it was harder to make a living now. Not many people wanted made-to-measure suits. They did alterations, patching up old clothes in return for vegetables, bread, eggs. I was alone in still looking well dressed when everyone in the streets was shabby.

I was ashamed of it at school, and tried to explain to my friends. They understood, but I could sense their jealousy. Then, gradually, they started asking for my address. It seemed I had friends I didn't know about.

I had plenty of good laughs with my own, real friends. Once, in the Underground, when everyone was crushed close together in the train, we drew in lipstick on the back of a German officer's uniform. And when he got out on the platform you could see all the passengers hiding their laughter. What a joke!

Germans. Germans everywhere, in all the streets, and signs in German too. We were occupied. Mother and Father were increasingly busy, because the parents of my new friends came to our shop as winter approached, to get their coats made fit to last another year. But these days, when they reached our shop with a few lumps of coal or some fruit at the bottom of their baskets, they found a special notice stuck to the window. It said JEWISH FIRM. 'Firm' was rather a grand word for Father and Mother's tiny shop still full of unclaimed items of property. Apart from them, it contained a sewing machine, a cutting-out table, an ironing board and a dummy in a blue suit in the window. JEWISHFIRM.

Why? Father, why did you believe those pigs? Why didn't you follow Yantel's example? You went on with your life just as before, while we were becoming more and more Jewish and worth less and less. We never saw Yantel again. He went away to hide, to fight. I'm sure he must have killed German soldiers. He was right, too. But why didn't you explain to me, Father? Why didn't you rebel, just a little?

You were proud of my end-of-term reports. You kissed them when you read them. Why were you so blind? I feel as if I understood things better than you did even then, better than Mother, who never liked to contradict you. I talked politics with my friends at school. We didn't discuss anything at home. I had to do my hour of piano practice, however, even in winter. Mother knitted me some mittens.

Why? Why didn't you express any rebellion at all when they said we couldn't own wireless sets, and they must be handed in at the Town Hall? Not that you did hand ours in, luckily. But you never said a word of hatred or anger or even annoyance. I just don't understand. You'll explain one day – won't you? You will, won't you?

I wish you knew how I feel sitting here, Father. I haven't eaten for two days. I'm not hungry anyway. I'm sitting in this classroom writing,

writing as fast as I can, to tell you, so you'll know, to explain things to you, to everyone, to the whole world – and I must be quick, I mustn't leave anything out, right up to the moment when we meet again. I want you. I want you both. I want to be held in your arms and weep, with joy or despair, I don't mind which.

'You're right, Jacob. The shop's not worth keeping on.'

One Sunday morning, with the assistance of Monsieur Herschl and Salomon the butcher, Father brought the sewing machine and the cutting-out table home. I wasn't allowed to help.

'Your hands, David, your hands! Suppose you injured your hands?'

I couldn't have cared less about my hands. I wanted to help you. And as you had so much to do, I secretly brought everything I could back to the flat.

And then I saw you cry, Mother, as you and I stood side by side on the opposite pavement, watching Father pull the iron shutter down. No more JEWISH FIRM. You couldn't see our name up over the door any more. Father simply lowered his head as we went home, without a word. Then there was a lot to do, reorganizing life in the flat. Customers would come there now; it wasn't particularly complicated.

And sure enough, they did come, and Mother and Father worked even harder once Jews were forbidden to be out of doors between eight in the evening and six in the morning.

What had we done to deserve it? Can anyone tell me that? Here I am all alone in this vast house, a kind of manor house, and only silence replies. We were Jewish. So what's the harm in that? We weren't even religious Jews. Hardly Jewish at all. I never set foot in a synagogue in my life. Mother and Father had a civil wedding ceremony at Montreuil Town Hall. If you exist, God, I don't believe in you. I hate you. I curse you. I despise you. I spit in your face. I'm sick of it all, I'd like to die, I'd like to lie here dying until you answer me. I want you to see how I'm bleeding inside, I want to make you reply, just with a word, a sign. Why?

Why did life stop? Why did my friends start discussing films I couldn't see any more? Why did Father forbid me to go to the cinema alone in the evening to see the main programme and the big film?

'It's the law, David. And if you obey the law you'll be all right,' he said. 'Nothing will happen then.'

It was true enough that nothing happened. Ever. As if life had stopped dead. There was nothing. I can't describe it. It was so boring, with the wireless turned low, issuing orders, playing music to soothe the nothingness, the great void. Father and Mother and I, and others like us, a great many of them, had no right to any kind of normal life in the evenings.

If we ever went out it would mean prison, a fine, or internment in a 'Jewish camp'. What did that mean? And where was it?

I pretended during break at school. Pretended to laugh, pretended I'd seen the film they were all talking about. I pretended. Until the day I realized what it meant to be a Jew, and that there was no need for explanations. Even Father couldn't have been in any uncertainty there. It was clear, visible, obligatory.

A yellow star to be worn by everyone Jewish over six years old, from 7 June 1942: We went meekly back to the police station as if we were going to the stake, to be given three stars each in return for a point from our clothing coupons. The policeman behind his desk handed out the stars without a word, as if he was afraid to look at us. And then, I don't know why, as we were about to leave, the Inspector himself called to us, and we went into his office. He asked Mother and Father to sit down. We must have looked blank. There was a photograph of Marshal Pétain on the wall.

'It's the law, Monsieur Grunbaum. Nothing I can do about it. I'm obliged to enforce it.' But there was a look of sympathy and of indignation on his face. 'It's the law. Well, if you just do as they say – and look, I'll be around to see you one of these days quite soon. Don't worry.'

He rose. We all rose. He shook hands with us.

'I won't forget about you.'

We left, feeling baffled.

But over the next few months we could see that a number of other people hadn't forgotten about us either.

## ENTRY FORBIDDEN
## TO JEWS
## ANTRITT FÜR JUDEN
## VERBOTEN

said the notices. Everything was forbidden. Not just cinemas, but public gardens and swimming baths too, absolutely everything, even the shops; we weren't allowed to go shopping except between three and four in the afternoon.

'Might as well starve to death and have done with it,' said Father, when he heard.

'Don't say that, Jacob,' said Mother. 'We'll manage, you know we will.'

We were visible with our stars, highly visible. But at the same time *they* wanted us to become invisible. Just the last coach of the Underground train.

When I went to school wearing my yellow star that first day, I heard murmurs. 'I say, I'd never have thought . . .' That was all. My friends talked to me just the same as before, in fact they were even a bit friendlier. But I remember going home that evening, and meeting an old gentleman with a walking stick, his head bent, going down the street the other way. He stopped right in front of me.

'Here, boy,' he said.

He took a coin out of his pocket and gave it to me. I looked into his eyes. 'Poor child,' he muttered as he walked on.

There were thousands of poor children like me. And hundreds of thousands of poor grown-ups. Jews. Jews. Jews. We recognized each other a long way off in the streets, in the Underground. I could spot the women who tried to hide the star behind their handbags, too. I knew all about it. At least, I thought I knew all about it until the day when unexpectedly – out of the blue, I swear it – there was a knock at the door.

Mother went to open it. It was the police inspector. The pleasant one, the one who had shaken hands with us at the station. He wanted a word with Father and Mother; he wanted to see their papers again.

'Leave us, David.'

I shut myself in one of the bedrooms. They were speaking in such low voices I couldn't hear a word. But I heard the slam of the door when he left.

Why? Why didn't you tell me anything that day? Why? I could have told you what to do. Certainly not send me off to sleep at the Bianchottis' that very evening, after you hit me. That's not what we ought to have done. You did what you thought best for me. And what about yourselves?

When I heard the screaming very early in the morning of 16 July, I went to the window, with Madame Bianchotti. There was a terrible, loud shrieking, and a whole crowd of policemen in the street. With all of her tiny strength, Madame Bianchotti put her hand over my mouth.

I don't know how to say the next bit. I don't want to. I can't. I will, though. My stomach heaves, my throat hurts. My head is going round and round, but I'll say it. I'll get it down even if I die writing it.

Madame Weiss was out in the street. Two policemen were pulling her along by her hair to make her go with them. She was weeping. She was calling for help. No one went to help her. I saw families coming out of the buildings: my friends, their little brothers and sisters. They followed their parents without a word. Silence. Just silence to drown out the noise Madame Weiss was making. And then I saw Father and Mother, carrying a suitcase, with two policemen, one on each side of them. I saw them raise their heads and look at my window. I saw that they had seen me, and they saw that I had seen them. Madame Bianchotti pressed her hand tighter and tighter against my mouth, to muffle any sound I might make. Father and Mother went away with the others, surrounded by policemen. Within ten minutes there wasn't a Jew left in our little neighbourhood except me.

Well, that's it. I've said it. Now I can die. Only I don't want to. Mother's eyes, turned towards me. Father's eyes, turned towards me. I suppose I'll see those eyes, those figures, for the rest of my life. My parents. My mother and father. I'm all alone. Come back. Don't leave me – you never said goodbye. I only saw you for a few seconds just before you turned the corner of the road, walking in line. A few seconds of eternity, during which Madame Bianchotti sobbed as she held me close, hugging me to her.

'They'll be back, David, don't you worry. They'll be back.'

From the window, I saw the windows opposite close again. I saw the curtains drawn. It was over. A quiet morning early in July, in a street without any history, but where my own story was just beginning.

Summoning up all my strength, I freed myself from Madame Bianchotti by knocking her to the floor. I raced downstairs in my pyjamas and ran after them blindly, going the wrong way. I hadn't seen anything, I told myself. I hadn't seen anything. Nothing had happened. I yelled.

'Mother! Mother – Father!'

Then I ran out of steam. I walked slowly back from the Porte de Montreuil. I was alone. Completely alone. I found myself back in Madame Bianchotti's arms. She couldn't speak. She cradled me like a baby, gently stroking my hair. I could have stayed there for hours, but Father had taught me to keep going, even when my eyes were full of tears.

'Madame Bianchotti, what am I going to do? It's all over, isn't it? It's all over. Once *they* realize I'm missing they'll come for me too. I must get away from here.'

I put my day clothes on, tearing off my star, and went downstairs, to go home. I hadn't noticed as I ran back upstairs, but there were seals on the doors. Two red wax seals, and a thread between them. I wasn't supposed to go into my own home. I tore the thread away and put my key in the lock. I broke in. Then I lay down on the dining-room floor. I've no idea how long I lay there weeping in the familiar smell of home, of Mother and Father. If I'd been a dog I could have followed them by their scent. But I was only a child.

I didn't yell, I just drummed my feet on the floor with rage. Pure rage, as impotent as it was strong. I ought to get out of here, because *they* would be back. I didn't want to. However, *they* had taken my parents away. *They* would take me too. It didn't take long to pack my case, cramming everything into it any old how. My things. What about theirs? Their things were there, in the wardrobe, in the chests of drawers, their presence everywhere. So, feeling like a thief, I took their wedding photograph, slipping it out of its frame. I put it in my suitcase. I would never, never part with it.

I slammed the door. I had no home any more. Just my life and a photograph.

It's here beside me now. I look at them. I smile at them. I have no tears left.

I'm just writing all this down like a robot.

Madame Bianchotti wanted to avenge her son. I never seemed to have seen her except in floods of tears, but now her eyes were perfectly dry. And her husband had stopped staring at that memorial photograph of their son and found his voice again.

'The pigs!' said Madame Bianchotti. 'The pigs! They had no right to do a thing like that.'

She had gone out to gather news of what was going on. Apparently thousands of people had been arrested all over Paris and the suburbs.

'You must stay here for a few days, and then, well, you wait and see, things will sort themselves out.'

And to be honest, things did sort themselves out. They always do, from day to day. I suppose they have to. But when you add up the result, the way I'm adding it up now, it's calculated either to send you crazy or make you determined to live at all costs. I don't know if you can actually choose which. There are times I think I'm crazy, or going crazy, but I know that the words on this page are really saying I've decided to live at any price. It's not a deliberate decision. It's some kind of force coming up from deep, deep down, and even stronger than grief.

Madame Bianchotti didn't leave me much time to think about my parents. Just a day, that was all. The day after their arrest. My own home was there, two floors down, and I couldn't go back to it. All my things were there. My books, my school work, my old teddy bears, carefully wrapped up, and my little lead racing cyclists. Nothing very grand, but it meant so much. I thought about those things all day long, lying on the dead man's bed. I'd avenge him too. In the middle of my savage thoughts I started sobbing. Father, Mother! Mother, Father! Where did *they* take you?

'First to the Marcelin Berthelot school, then by coach to the Winter Velodrome,' Madame Bianchotti told me.

She had been out and about in Paris all day, and gleaned a lot of information. There had just been another raid, but it was an almost total failure. People had been on the alert.

And then, unasked, she handed me an identity card. A false one, though it looked perfectly genuine and had the photograph out of my old card. But I had changed my name, and the word JEW wasn't there. I was called Daniel Larcher. I stared at it, unable to believe my eyes. How on earth had she done it? I had known she was planning something, because she'd asked me for my papers before going out, so she said, to do her shopping.

'There are still some decent people around in France,' Madame Bianchotti told me, simply. 'Some really decent people.'

That was all. She must have promised to keep the details secret.

Now that I knew where my parents were, I kept trying to think of ways to rescue them. But what could I do? How could I get to them? Madame Bianchotti was keeping me a prisoner.

I'm sorry I wrecked your dead son's room when you locked me in there, Madame Bianchotti. I'm sorry I broke the crucifix and tore up your photo of Bertrand, and opened the window and shouted that I wanted my parents back. I'm sorry I smashed the big mirror in the wardrobe, and tore up your son's shirts and suits. I know you've forgiven me though. You even opened the door yourself before I smashed it in with the chair I'd already broken, and the marble top from the bedside table I was using to hammer away at the lock.

Then I flung myself into your arms. It was all the warmth I could beg for. My body was freezing, even though I was running with sweat. You comforted me without a word of reproach.

It was goodbye to Montreuil, my home town, not my home any more now. Carrying a small suitcase, I followed Madame Bianchotti to the Gare du Nord railway station. All the way she made me keep repeating my new name and my new life history. The Germans took no notice of me when they came down the train checking papers. But the real surprise was when I got out of the train. It seemed I was still in Montreuil. As if my home town stuck to my skin. Only this was a different Montreuil, of course. The notice on the station platform said, in large letters, MONTREUIL-sur-MER, Montreuil-on-Sea.

It had been a long, long journey with Madame Bianchotti, an old lady all dressed in black, in mourning for her son. She didn't tell me I was about to fall into the hands of a whole lot of other people dressed in black, like her, but not because they were in mourning.

We came to a huge, tall black building beside a church.

Madame Bianchotti rang the bell by the big front door. A priest opened it.

'I'd like to see the Father Superior, please. Tell him his sister is here.'

The man in black let us in. Automatically, I took Madame Bianchotti's hand. She was as surprised as I was. And only now, at the end of our long journey, did she smile at me.

'They'll see you're all right here. You've nothing to fear, trust me!'

How could I tell her I didn't trust anyone any more, anyone at all? Not even the man in the cassock who came to meet us. He kissed Madame Bianchotti lightly, but I could tell he was pleased to see her, and curious.

'Come along!'

I followed them under the arches of the main courtyard, up to an office on the first floor. There was a terrifying silence in this place, which I now discovered was a school. A grammar school? That would be something familiar. I had to wait outside the Father Superior's door, with my suitcase on the floor beside me.

Montreuil-sur-Mer. Montreuil-sur-Mer. Slowly, tears rose to my eyes. *Mer*, sea, sounded just like *mère*, mother. Mother!

Madame Bianchotti kissed me hard, very hard, her hands on my cheeks.

'You're safe now, David. Do whatever my brother tells you. He knows your story. He knows all about it. And about your parents – I'll do everything I can.'

And she left. I felt the pressure of a hand on my shoulder. It didn't stay there long, but there was warmth in the gesture.

Then Madame Bianchotti's small figure moved away from me towards the front door.

I'm glad I gave you so much trouble, Father Superior, I'm glad I didn't co-operate so you could help me to help myself. I know you didn't actually set out to humiliate me, but that's what you did. I felt such hatred in my heart – I still feel it now. I suppose I owe you an apology for some things, but that's as far as I'll go. You did as you thought best. I did as I had to.

You made me go to church every Sunday, bobbing up and down in the pew. You made me say your Lord's Prayer. You wanted to change me so I wouldn't be like myself any more. But you didn't know that in my suit pocket, like a forgotten handkerchief, I still had my yellow star to tell me who I was.

I had to say prayers before school every morning. I had to listen to your sermons telling us to give thanks to the Lord. I listened. Thank you, Lord, for taking my parents away from me. Thank you, Lord, for sending me into hiding just to stay alive. Thank you, Lord, for making sure I don't get letters from anyone. Thank you, Lord, for dumping me in the rat-hole where I looked round the class the first few times I was called Daniel Larcher for the idiot who didn't know his own name. Thank you, Lord, for landing me in that holy prison of a boarding school where no news came in from outside except on Sunday evenings, when the lucky boys who had local friends to take them out for the day came back.

That's enough thanks. That's enough compassion. I hated you, Father Superior, for making me sit through those Religious Instruction lessons when you went on about the Jews murdering Christ. I knew enough to know your Christ was Jewish himself, so why all the lies? I hated you for trying to convert me.

For the first month, I was too badly shaken to fight back. I soon got over that. Death was certainly waiting outside. But there was another kind of death in your school, in the shelter of those high walls where the only reality was things with names like locative, dative, ablative, and other ridiculous stuff – while outside, the Nazis were laying down the law. 'Jesus wept, Jesus wept, Jesus wept,' I kept saying to myself all through Mass, hating your Jesus Christ.

Remember when you summoned me to see you and explained that I had to behave like the others, I mustn't attract attention, or there could be serious repercussions? All those precautions! As if I didn't know it. Forty in a dormitory. Find the Jew! It would have been a new game. And he wouldn't have been recognized by his nose so much as by his tears flowing like milk and honey in the land that kept cropping up in those sermons. Then you told me about Confession and Communion, and you were on the point of telling me about baptism too. You seemed to like the idea that everyone was on the wrong side of God.

Perhaps I'm being unfair. Perhaps I'm accusing you of intentions you didn't really have. But I have to let off steam somehow.

I felt crazy. You made me feel crazy. Every evening after prayers, bedtime and lights out, I thought of getting my revenge. Yes, I know you saved my life, but only to make me die even more horribly. I felt I was dying of the thoughts going round and round in my head and always homing in on my parents' photograph. I would go and get it out of the little cupboard at the foot of my bed. Without waking anyone, I would take it out and look at it. Although what could I see in the dark? Everything. Every tiny detail. Father on the left, Mother on the right. The look on their faces, the clothes they wore. Father and Mother, always there. I knew the picture by heart. On those evenings when I felt saddest of all I didn't have the heart to go and get it out, but then, hard as I tried, there was no way I could make their faces appear before my mind's eye. Impossible. It was impossible, I tried and tried until I was exhausted. I had to be shaken awake in the morning. And then suddenly, unexpectedly, their faces did come back to me, filling my day with tears.

Then came anger: a vast and carefully nurtured anger.

It was Sunday, and Mass again. I went up to the altar with my hand on my chest. No one was expecting it. They all turned to look at me. I could feel them looking. The priests dared not stop me. Before the ceremony began, I turned towards all those people whose names I didn't know, whose existence I didn't want to acknowledge. I took my hand away from my chest and let my yellow star splatter its filth all over them. Without a word, I went back to my bed in the dormitory.

It was good to touch that yellow star, clumsily pinned in place with a safety pin stolen from the laundry room. A badge of shame which made me myself again.

I wasn't crazy any more, not now I'd made my crazy gesture. I lay stretched on my bed, lying on my back, breathing quietly, with my boots on the bedspread. Nothing could happen to me now. I knew who I was again.

I still remember lying there breathing slowly,

deeply, as I stroked my little bit of cloth.

For the first time, Mother and Father, I thought of you with happiness. I wasn't used to happiness. The yellow star reunited us after all those months. You had been wearing yours when *they* came to arrest you. I wore mine too now, the way I used to when you were still there. That morning was full of warmth. I was with you again.

The Father Superior, in his bare, polished office, didn't dare order me to take 'that thing' off again. I saw his angry eyes. He saw mine, even angrier.

Then he rose and came over to me. He ran his hand over my close-cropped hair. I pulled away, but he had been too quick for me.

'I shall pray for you, David. You cannot be one of us, not after today. But I will not abandon you.'


Is the Father Superior still praying for me, I wonder? Now, this very moment? No, he'll have forgotten me. But if he ever did keep that promise, I'd like him to add some other names to the name he gave me back. He can pray for them if he likes, if it does any good, if that's what he believes. Myself, I just think about them, that's all, in the silence and the sunlight falling into this classroom. He can write their names in the great book where God records good and bad deeds. He told me about it himself. Maybe God won't have enough ink in his pen. He can pray God has enough bottles of Waterman Blue. All I have is a black pencil which is wearing down too fast, and these sheets of squared paper.

However, it's fair to say that the Father Superior didn't abandon me. Not entirely. I wasn't allowed to go to prayers, and they kept me in the infirmary for a week. The others might have been contaminated by me and my star.

A week when I was free to be myself, wearing my own clothes, the ones I'd stolen from home, made by Mother. No more blue uniform and school overall. I can't say how happy I was to put those clothes on again and catch the smell of home on myself. I'd have known it anywhere. I sniffed at my clothes like a human dog. I still had something left of my past. I was free. I didn't have to attend lessons. I was going to leave that place. I knew I was. I even ventured to lie about on the lawn in the main courtyard. But slowly, fear crept back. What was I going to do once I had my suitcase in my hand, and I stood outside the boarding school all alone?

The Father Superior came over to me one fine afternoon as I was idly throwing pebbles in the cloisters, one by one, feeling bored to death.

'You're leaving, David. Everything's ready now. I told you I wouldn't forget you.'

I was overcome by panic again. I felt like clinging to you, Father Superior, so that you'd protect me. I know you could see that in my eyes. I know because your own became kind and friendly. I think you respected me then. You understood the distress beneath the pride of a boy who had defied you. I felt like clutching your cassock. All I did was clench my fists.

I followed you, without a word from you, to your office. The door was open.

A man stood there, straight-backed, looking at the photograph of Marshal Pétain, and the crucifix just below it.

A man in a well-cut dark suit. You went in. I couldn't cross the threshold. The man still didn't turn round. The suitcase you had told me to pack stood at his feet.

Dreadful images came back to me. *They* had gone looking for my parents. *He* had come looking for me. I swear I didn't tremble. *He* was never going to get me. I took off in a split second, making for the stairs. I jumped down four steps at a time, holding the banisters. I jumped another four steps and fell head first, half stunning myself.

I opened my eyes. The man with my suitcase was standing in front of me, while the Father Superior held my head up. I was all right. I scrambled to my feet. The man with the suitcase held me firmly by the wrist, almost breaking it.

'It's all over now. There's nothing to fear.'

He had a moustache, and short-sighted eyes behind big glasses.

'*Ourem Kind*,' he said.

Then I understood. The magical language Father and Mother used to speak rang in my ears. The man with my suitcase was speaking Yiddish, like them. 'Poor child,' he had said.

I pressed close to him. He would protect me from all evil.

Thank you, although I don't know your name. And thank you, Father Superior, for handing me over to him.

He took my suitcase, placed his hand on my shoulder, and then we were out on the other side of those high walls.

Free. Free at last. A long, slow walk to the station while a question I dared not put went round and round in my head. I looked at the plate-glass windows, the bicycles, the occasional cars, the queues outside the shops. And then the all-important question came out, in a very small voice, just before we reached the station.

'Are you taking me back to my parents, sir? Have they been found?'

He didn't pretend not to have heard me. He put my suitcase down. He took me by the shoulders. He looked me straight in the eye.

'Listen carefully, David. There will be no lies between us. I don't know where your parents are, or what has become of them. We shall do all we can to find them. But it's your own life we're concerned with now. I am taking you to a safe place. I'm Jewish, like you, and my job is saving Jewish children. You mustn't ask my name. Forget the place where you used to live, your home, your parents. Save your life. Your own life. We only get one.'

I shall never forget what you said, though I don't know your name. You had a moustache and a nondescript accent. You were right, in spite of my tears and the lemonade you bought me at the station buffet. I had to live. Keep living until I died.

As for the rest – well, my other thoughts surfaced again in the train to Paris, when I had to show my genuine-looking false identity card to the Nazi soldiers checking papers again.

I remember leaning my head against your shoulder, feeling great warmth.

Paris. We'd be in Paris in a few hours. Montreuil, my old home, was only a few stations away by Underground train. But I wasn't going there. My street was out of bounds, my home was out of bounds, the shop was shut up. Oh sir, couldn't we go a little way round, please, just a tiny little detour? It won't take long. They may have come back. And even if they aren't back I could say hello to Madame Bianchotti. No. It was all out of bounds, I knew that. And I had no tears left.

I fell asleep with my head still against your shoulder.

I wish I could do that now, this very moment. If I could put my head down on my arms at the school desk where I'm sitting and go to sleep, I would. But I'm not going to stop writing until I've got it all down. I can see the words dancing before my eyes.

I'm not going to stop. My writing is crammed close on the pages. I must get it all down as fast as I can, and then I can sleep . . .

I didn't get it all down. I couldn't keep my promise. I don't know what happened. I woke up a little while ago to find myself lying on the floor. How long did I spend asleep there? No way of telling. All I know is it's nearly morning. I went to the kitchen and ate three fried eggs and a huge slice of dry bread. Outside the sun is rising. There's white dew in the garden. It looks beautiful. I've picked up my pencil again. It's cold. I went up to the dormitory to find two blankets. One to drape over my shoulders, one to wrap round my legs.

You brought me here by way of Paris, man whose name I don't know. We crossed the city from one station to another. Then a wait, with memories crowding back thick and fast, until I thought, briefly, of making my escape.

It was just then you looked at me. I know you guessed what I was thinking. And I saw a tear behind your thick glasses.

Perhaps *they* took your own people away too, all your family? Perhaps you were thinking much the same as I was in the second-class waiting room? Perhaps you had a wife, and children, and you didn't know where they were? But I had no right to ask you questions.

All I remember is that I put my hand on yours, and you didn't withdraw it.

( 62 )

Did you perhaps want to escape too, I wonder, and see the street where you used to live and your old home again?

What about mine? Suppose other people had taken over my room, my things, Mother and Father's things? Suppose . . . ?

And the tears rose to my eyes again. I didn't try to hold them back. It did no good, just made my throat hurt. I knew that. I had plenty of experience by now. You might as well let the tears flow. Anyway, it's not true that real men don't cry.

Your glasses were all misty. Only people who aren't men don't cry, people who aren't human beings at all. People without any feelings. I'm almost a man myself now, and no one will ever stop me crying.

It was a horrible wait. But at last it was time to set off, going south.

Why didn't you tell me your name, even a false name? I could have talked to you in those long hours we spent together on the wooden seats of the train compartment, travelling towards Brive.

I'm not sure why, but you looked as if you might be called Max. So you're Monsieur Max to me.

So many things to say, but we said none of them. We just exchanged a few words in the corridor, in a low voice. Questions about my age, my school work, what I wanted to do when I grew up. There were so many words that couldn't be spoken. Simple words, the very simplest: your father, your mother, your wife, your children. We spoke none of them out loud. But we said it all in the language of the eyes. Even short-sighted people can speak that language. Thank you, Monsieur Max. I even managed to laugh once, I can't remember what about, and I saw your face light up. I'd just laughed.

Laughter and tears mean life. You laughed too.

And the sound of laughter – the first laughter I'd felt like hearing in a long time – welcomed me here after a long bus journey with Monsieur Max.

Meanwhile, at G., both of us sitting at the back of the bus, he had told me where we were going.

'We shall arrive in quarter of an hour's time. You'll be really free then. You can call yourself David again and be as Jewish as you like. You're going to a home for Jewish children. I shall be off again to find other children. You're not a child yourself any more; you're grown up. You must have aged a great deal in a very few months, but never forget: keep going, keep going to the very end. And then, well, perhaps you'll see your parents again.'

The bus stopped outside a village shop. Monsieur Max and I were the only passengers to get out. Suddenly I understood his last words, and the silence he had preserved throughout our journey. Of course I was going to see my parents again! That was the surprise he was keeping for me. A wonderful surprise! I swear I had never before walked as fast as I did along that road from the village, climbing uphill into a wood of chestnut trees.

I knew they would be there at the end of the road.

'And then, well, perhaps you'll see your parents again.'

I blotted the 'perhaps' out of my mind. I *was* going to see them again! Only a few hundred metres more, soon after the place where the road branched, and a high-banked lane led through the undergrowth.

Far away, on a little rise, I saw a building of pink stone. I was sure. Quite sure. I started running towards my parents. They were there! They were there! Only a few more steps now. Their arms ready to welcome me. Only a small flight of stone stairs to climb, and I could open the door to untold happiness.

Untold grief, in fact. They weren't there.

You deceived me, Monsieur Max. You were like all the others.

All right, I know I'm being unfair. I know I really deceived myself; it was my only hope.

'And then, well, perhaps you'll see your parents again.'

'Perhaps.' Such a stupid but perfectly normal hope. I don't hate you for it, Monsieur Max. Not any more. I love you. You were my companion for three exhausting days. Three days of comfort and wild hope.

And then a huge house, but with no parents waiting for me. Just the sound of laughter and singing, coming from I didn't know where.

Monsieur Max rejoined me.

'Here we are,' he said. 'Now you'll see.'

I saw.

A small woman with remarkable eyes had come to meet us. A small woman who kissed Monsieur Max, and unexpectedly took my hand, calling me by my first name.

'Come along, David.'

How did she know my name?

Monsieur Max had gone into the house. I was left with Madame Lonia. I didn't try withdrawing my hand from hers. I was staggering with weariness, unable to understand, unable to let all my disappointment out – though the word 'disappointment' is too weak for what I felt. I was knocked out. But the small woman guided me out into the garden with her small, firm hand.

'See that flower, David? Lovely, isn't it?'

I couldn't have cared less about your flower, Madame Lonia. What kind of substitute for parents is a flower? Flowers are for putting on graves. I could have stuffed your little yellow flower down your throat. But you seemed to think no end of it. Then you bent down to pick it. You gave it to me.

'Here, David. Welcome to our house.'

There was such sincerity in your voice, with its slight Russian accent, that I sat down on the ground, holding the flower, my eyes suddenly wet. You sat down beside me, waiting patiently for me to recover my sight, my life, and look at the yellow flower, at my hands, at the huge oak tree in the meadow and the first bushes of the wood at the end

( 66 )

of the garden. And waiting for my glance to meet yours again, Lonia. You said I could call you just Lonia.

'Real life begins now, David. You have nothing to hide here, and nothing to hide from yourself. No more lies. You can forget all the stories and secrets and invented things you've had to tell other people, and yourself, about your life. You're Jewish here, the son of Jewish parents. It's an honour, David, although it ought to be regarded just as something perfectly normal.'

And then Lonia went on, while I fell asleep on the grass, freed from all those months of make-believe, false identity, false everything. Perhaps you couldn't sleep until you were really yourself again, not unless you were simply worn out. I felt a kiss. I didn't start. I was happy. I wasn't even thinking of my parents any more.

When I woke up Lonia was still there, sitting on the grass in her blue dress. She was not alone any more. I was surrounded by children of all ages, sitting in a circle, waiting. As soon as I opened my eyes they started singing a song, in quiet voices.

> Good day to you, good day we say,
> Be welcome on this happy day
> To our work and to our play.

I shall always remember those ridiculous words – ridiculous when I write them down, but they were genuine and seriously meant. And that silly little tune, with the children singing in accents which reminded me of my father's voice. I was shaking. I had gooseflesh. But I didn't shed a tear.

There were two little girls, twin sisters, with plaits, and a large, hairy boy in shorts.

> Good day to you, good day we say,
> Be welcome on this happy day
> To our work and to our play.

They were the only ones I noticed. I got to know the others gradually, as the days went by. The children accompanied me to the flight of stone steps up to the house. Lonia followed her little flock, smiling.

'What's your name?'

'Where do you come from?'

'How did you escape?'

'Where are your parents?'

'Have you had anything to eat?'

'Did the Germans torture you?'

Ida. Rachel. Samuel. Hélène. Your names come back to me, one by one. Maurice. Hanna . . . All of you, though I sometimes hated you, sometimes felt like hitting you. All of you who laughed with me – your names are a long list that I ought to write down in order. I don't feel up to it. You should be here now, with me. I'm alone.

You bombarded me with questions. I felt quite dizzy.

'Did the Gestapo get your parents?'

'They killed my brother in the middle of the street, but he died killing one of *them*.'

You had so many things to tell a newcomer who had just arrived in the quiet countryside of the Lot valley, to find people there who had suffered even more than he had.

Yet your grief never wiped out mine. We shared our unhappiness, which somehow made it more bearable.

How was I to answer your questions? I didn't even know you yet.

What could I say to you, Perla, the smallest of all, just five years old? You grabbed me by the shorts I was wearing and tugged hard with your tiny hands, to make me look at you.

'Hey,' you asked me, 'did you see my mummy where you've come from?'

You were the only one I felt like answering that day. I could have answered you with the same question. 'Hey, Perla, did you see my parents where you've come from?'

I was too tired to think. I was still clutching the yellow flower. The crowd of children surged round me as if they were all, both large and small, carrying me up to the first floor to deposit me on my own bed in the boys' dormitory. *My* bed.

I didn't count the beds until I woke up again. Ten beds. Ten children. Two more empty beds were waiting.

They had let me sleep a long time. How long?

The walls were bare. The yellow flower stood in a glass on my bedside table. To keep it alive. And – oh, I'd forgotten him. I had to say goodbye.

Where was Monsieur Max?

'He's gone to rescue other children,' Lonia told me, in her office next to the kitchen.

Her eyes could not lie.

I think he came up to the dormitory before leaving and kissed my forehead.

I shall meet him again one day, and kiss him back, and all the other children he's saved will kiss him too.


I was in Lonia's office. It had a bed in one corner. A desk, a chair, a vase of flowers and a pleasant smell of wax polish.

Lonia sat down on her bed. I sat on the chair.

'Did you sleep well, David? You needed a good sleep. Now, before you see the others again, there's something I must tell you. We are free here, but we have to help each other. Mutual aid. Do you understand, David? Mutual aid is very important.'

I understood. She spoke so emphatically, in her lilting accent.

'Each of us here depends on the others. You are one of the eldest, so once you've got to know them I'd like you to look after the little ones, help them, tell them stories, make up games for them. I trust you. Indeed, I trust all of you.'

I took in her words, feeling rather solemn. I was sure there was no evil here now, only grief, a great grief which might, perhaps, pass over.


Lonia made me feel that. I don't know what she

really expected of me. I knew what I expected of her. And now she's gone too.

I put my pencil down a moment ago, to go and look at her office. The bed is made. The bunch of flowers on the table is faded. I'll pick a new one. Lonia rose at six every morning, polished her own office floor, and was there when we got up to give us her life-saving smile. Shall I ever see her again? Shall I ever hear her voice, a voice that sang even when she was severe, or issuing a warning? Someone tell me we'll meet again.

If I close my eyes very tight, perhaps I shall hear her say so herself.

The silence of the house makes me afraid. And yet there's nothing to fear. The worst has happened. What does anything matter now? All the same I'm afraid. Nothing more can frighten me, but I'm still afraid. Afraid to say what has happened. Afraid of my solitude, the absence of noise, laughter, tears, accents from all the countries of Europe, hidden away in the valley of the Lot here: Lithuanian, German, Austrian, Czech, Hungarian, Flemish, even the accent of the South of France. I miss your voices more than anything else. Hélène, I really disliked your accent, but I wish you'd come back and shout in my ears. Keep shouting until you deafen me! But come back, do, and tell me again how you crossed unknown territory on foot to find peace here in the middle of the war. Tell me. Tell me. I need to be told stories, any stories, so I won't be left alone with *my* story, I can't stand that.

Quick, someone talk to me, like Lonia in the evenings when she came into our dormitory to tell us a story. Of course I made myself out very grown-up and above such things. Little children's stories weren't my cup of tea. Did she know how I listened, though, never missing a word?

She would sit on a chair in the middle of the room, telling tales of another world. She had a book in her hand, but she never looked at it. Her eyes went from face to face. The smallest children hid under the bedclothes. Every evening there would be a story about a prince, a princess, magic animals, or real children with real troubles who had lost their parents but found them again. Lonia heard the sobs and dried the children's tears at the end, going from bed to bed with a kindly word, like a sweet for the night.

I followed the adventures of Sindbad the Sailor, Ulysses, Aladdin and his wonderful lamp, Tom Thumb. At the end of the story Tom Thumb has made his fortune and goes home to his parents. I shed tears myself, and Lonia knew it. Perhaps I wasn't as grown-up as all that.

I shall remember the story of the brigands all my life, though. It scared me. It scared me so much that it used to wake me in the night, months and months before I really did grow up and a different sort of story started waking me in the night, with feelings of pleasure instead.

Yet the story of the brigands was about a little

girl. I don't remember its beginning or its end. I wasn't especially interested in all that. What I remember is that this little girl goes on a journey and is given a letter to deliver when she arrives. She doesn't know what the letter says, but it contains orders to have her beheaded as soon as she has delivered it. It still makes my flesh creep. I can remember Lonia's voice telling it perfectly. And I'm afraid. Afraid of a fairy story when I've lived through something really horrible, and I have to write it down, and here comes that little girl and her letter confusing everything. I don't understand. I don't understand it at all. If I ever have children I shall never tell them the story of that little girl. Anyway I don't know the whole of it.

But what on earth is it doing coming into my mind now? The hell with that stupid story barging in, holding me up.

And what use are these bits of paper and scraps of stories anyway? What use is all this hard work when there's nothing at all I can do about it, absolutely nothing. I shall stop writing. I'm going to sleep. What's the hurry to tell a story that doesn't interest anyone, nobody cares about it, it will never be any use for anything? Well, I know I *shall* finish it because I swore I would. I promised you, Mother and Father, I promised I'd write it down for you to see when we meet again. But I know we never will meet again. That's just about certain. The more time goes by, the less hope there is. Sleep. I want to sleep. Why go on plaguing myself to death when *they* couldn't do it? And they had plenty of ways to kill me. I'm going to sleep and forget. I want to forget. I shall rock myself to sleep, all alone. I know a place where I could go to weep, and talk, but I won't until I've finished this, told the whole story and kept my word. And then life can start again.

I woke all of a sudden, but found I couldn't move. My whole body was a block of solid marble. I couldn't reach out my hand or move my legs.

A face was bending over mine. A familiar face. My arms couldn't reach out to it or go round its neck. I saw Monsieur Rigal's big moustache. I must have looked funny lying on my back like that, eyes wide open, staring at him. He was sitting on a chair, waiting for me to wake up. Looking at me with his big, sad, kind eyes. There was the trace of a tear on his cheek. He quickly wiped it away with his handkerchief. Then he took off his policeman's cap and mopped his forehead.

'Tell me what you want to do, David lad. I'll do anything I can, anything. I was just passing, see, thought I'd see if there was any mushrooms, and then I said to myself you might have come back here.' His voice was gravelly. 'Disgusting it is, what they did.'

You didn't even need to say what you thought of it. It showed on your unshaven face, your drawn features – and you were always such a jovial sort of person.

You gave way first and collapsed, sobbing, into

my arms. The numbness was wearing off, and I put them round you. With my hand on your back I could feel the choking sobs going through you. Me, David, aged fifteen, comforting a big, strong, middle-aged man of fifty! Ridiculous really, but who cares?

Being unexpectedly woken up like that and seeing a man who didn't try to hide his grief, a normal human being, helped me pull myself together.

'Please don't be upset, Monsieur Rigal, you did all you could. It was nothing to do with you. And crying won't help now. Look at me, am I crying?'

I saw his large curly head lift, straighten up with dignity, and glance apologetically at me. Then, without a word, he took a large piece of bread and a sausage from the pocket of his baggy corduroy jacket, produced his knife, and shared the food between us.

We chewed slowly. He was sitting on Maurice's bed. Maurice used to scream in the night, every night. He couldn't remember anything about it in the morning.

I miss your screaming, Maurice, even if I often felt like smothering you with your pillow to make you shut up.

Monsieur Rigal was waiting for me to say something to make him feel better about showing what he regarded as weakness. All I could give was a smile to wipe the slate clean. I saw a smile of his own begin to dawn, uncertainly. And we both shrugged our shoulders at the same moment.

'Look, I can't leave you here, lad. Come home with me. The wife will look after you. There's plenty to eat, don't you worry. We'll do all right!'

Thank you, Monsieur Rigal. I owe you my life. But I have to bring that part of it to an end by myself now, in this empty house. And afterwards . . .

I wasn't afraid of anything or anyone now. I once used to find our local policeman Monsieur Rigal rather alarming when I went into the village, because of his way of talking to himself when slightly the worse for drink. Now I took his arm to show him over the house, room by room.

The girls' dormitory next door, several teddy bears still sleeping in the rumpled beds. Bedside tables crammed with little treasures: dolls, mascots, precious letters, photographs of people whose identity I didn't want to guess.

The big bathroom with its row of taps. Toothbrushes in glasses, and the soap drying up.

The kitchen where Madame Salviac was always hard at work from first thing in the morning. I had already been in there, and the remains of my meal were still on the table.

From the kitchen window you could see the vegetable garden which we watered every evening, to a rota. The beans and lettuces that nobody would pick now. It would all dry up. To think of all those watering cans we'd passed from hand to hand, singing! It was hard work for the little ones, but they were so keen to please Lonia they wouldn't let anyone help them. Like her, they were all for collective effort. Where is she? I want to know. Where is she?

Of course, Monsieur Rigal, following me in silence, couldn't know the significance of every untidily jettisoned object – one glance from Lonia would have had it back in its proper place in no time at all. Sarah's scarf. She was so fond of it. There it was in the big dining room, thrown down on a chair. I know the whole thing was so awful that the details wouldn't interest you, Monsieur Rigal. But to me those insignificant details meant my life, our life. Insignificant details, glimpsed in passing. The piano there, standing against the wall . . .

One reason why I'm writing this at all is because of the piano. But for the piano – well, I don't know.

Mother, Father, I started by disobeying Lonia, but I couldn't help it. The moment I saw that piano I headed for it, instead of taking my turn to help in the kitchen. I remembered my music lessons from the old lady with the hairy chin and the metronome – the overtime you did to pay for them. I played Clementi's sonatinas for you, or rather I tried to, because my fingers had stiffened up and the sound of wrong notes filled the air. I slammed my hands angrily down on the black and white keys.

I hadn't noticed Lonia come in.

'Losing your temper won't do any good. How marvellous to be able to play a musical instrument and be able to share something beautiful! Try again, David, and make it as good as possible.'

So I did try again, for her, for you, so that I could feel you here with me. And the whole little colony came and stood around me while I tried an easier, quieter tune: a little study for a beginner. When they all applauded, delighted, I realized they had fully accepted me.

'Hey, David, will you teach me to play the piano too?' asked little Perla.

I picked her up and kissed her.

'David, I want a word with you about the piano,' said Lonia. 'But all in good time.'

You didn't know any of that, Monsieur Rigal, I think you just guessed at a few bits, although our eyes never once met all through our tour of inspection.

You saw the big map of Europe in Lonia's office, and the flags she moved about on it every day. How did she know where to move them? Perhaps people like Monsieur Max, coming and going, brought her news.

Once a week she made us sit down on the floor, and told us things that brought us closer to our parents. Those little flags showed the landings in Italy and the Allied advance.

'Soon there won't be a single Nazi left.'

Without imagining any details, I dreamed of the happy ending Lonia said was coming soon. I loved her for giving me hope. Well, it's gone now, along with her, but she did so much for me. Lonia – your name's magic, your words were magic.

'And then the Soviet soldiers will march on Berlin too,' she told us. 'Never forget what the Communists have done for you. Later, when it's all over, we shall rebuild a free and happy France.'

She looked at us, suddenly realizing she had forgotten she was talking to children, and she found an excuse to change the subject, telling Maurice in a different tone of voice to stop picking his nose.

I was the oldest of us, and Lonia must have known from the laughter in my eyes that she hadn't fooled *me*. But I felt kindly towards her Communists, indeed I loved them because they would usher in a better world where everyone worked for others, and there would never be any more wars.

Tell me about the Communists again, Lonia, talk to me, tell me what the future will be like, talk about bread and roses and love and friendship. Talk to me, please, however far away you are. I need your voice, I need your certainties, I need your love.

Finally we got back to the classroom where I'm writing this now, and where I used to help the little ones with their reading and writing when I came back from school in the evenings. I had other things on my mind, but I did it.

'You see, Monsieur Rigal? The place is empty. Nothing left. Nothing left at all.'

The old man looked at me helplessly.

'Look, David lad, I'll come back and see you tomorrow. I may have some news by then. And

I'll bring you some food as well, of course.'

Lonia, who gave us so much love, may not really have known very much about it, or perhaps she'd forgotten. She kept talking about love; we knew her maxims off by heart, even the youngest of us. So why wouldn't she allow love its place, why was she so angry, why did she frighten us so and humiliate Maurice and Hanna? What crime had they committed? She found out one day when she was inspecting the rooms. The rest of us all knew about it; there was nothing wrong, it was perfectly normal. The two of them held hands in country dancing, and Hanna always picked Maurice for a partner. They stuck together when we went for walks in the woods, too, speaking volumes with their eyes.

Lonia summoned us all to the classroom one evening after supper. That was most unusual, and had never happened before.

For a moment we thought the war was over. We started crying and hugging each other for no reason at all, just because it was suddenly too much for us, and the thing we'd been hoping for for years had suddenly, unexpectedly, come true. We cried more than we laughed. The twins sat down on the floor and howled.

'Daddy – Mummy! It's over! They'll come and get us.'

But Lonia looked too solemn, too grave for that. This was something serious. Not a happy occasion, anyway. We filed into the classroom and sat down, sniffing slightly. She went up on the platform. From her pocket, she produced a letter she had already opened. In silence fit for a torture chamber, she slowly extracted a page torn from a school exercise book, and without warning she began to read it aloud.

From the way she spoke the words, holding the letter away from her as if it were infected by the plague, you'd have thought it contained untold horrors. But it was nothing except little loving words, sweet as the sort of thing I'd like to hear myself, remembering them. Tender and awkward, ending with Maurice sending Hanna a kiss on the mouth. 'A real kiss, not like in the cinema. I love you, Hanna.' Then Lonia showed us the sheet of paper, which had a carefully drawn heart on it.

Why did Lonia have to hurt them like that? Why did Hanna blush fiery red and then start sobbing? Why did Maurice look at us all as if apologizing? Apologizing for what? They'd done nothing wrong. But Lonia tormented them in front of us. It was unbearable.

The little ones listened without really understanding. I know what I felt about it: I felt like running up to her to snatch the letter away and give it back to Maurice. She had no right, no right at all. Her harsh, angry, wounding words were so unjust. I knew they were. I imagine the others did too, but Lonia really scared us. Does she remember what she said now? Does she remember the horrible things she said, all in the name of Love? Does she remember how she forced Maurice to own up?

He had to get to his feet, look at us, and say he was sorry for the shocking things he'd done – which were only part of life itself. Where was the harm in loving someone, or wanting some of the warmth we all missed? Touching another person's warm lips? But to big-hearted, cold-hearted Lonia love meant friendship, mutual aid, solidarity and so on. Not a word about our bodies. Not a word about the secret feelings that troubled us at night, in the day, as we read. We owed ourselves to the community, full stop.

What came over you that day, Lonia?

Why the blackmail to make Maurice own up?

'And if the guilty person – whose identity I know – will not identify himself, I shall have to turn him out of our community as someone unworthy of the ideals we cherish.'

Did she realize just what she was saying? Maurice would have left us. Hanna, having found a tiny bit of warmth, would have been deserted once again.

It sounded so awful that Marcel put his hands over his ears and rushed out of the room, crying.

Lonia had no right to do that. Yes, she comforted Maurice afterwards, yes, she read us a lecture, but she wounded me too. She made me a liar, and I hadn't been a liar before. I hold that against her. On the other hand, that evening saved my life.

When she accused Maurice, Lonia was accusing me too, though she didn't know it. I was writing love letters as well. And receiving them. I hid them in a shoe-box buried at the end of the garden, in the undergrowth where no one ever went. Whenever I could get away I went to reread them again and again, because the words in them were so sweet and warm and soothing. There was someone thinking of me, just me, and maybe some day we'd get married.

Claire. This is the first time since the terrible thing happened that I've written your name. But you're always there, in my mind, in my body. At first I thought of running straight to you, laying my head on your breast, holding you tight in my arms, to draw help and comfort from you. I could go and read your letters now. But I swore. I swore not to move from here until I've told a story I can hardly bear to tell. And then perhaps – no, certainly – I shall go to you and collapse. Your parents will know; well, never mind. There won't be anything to hide any more. We'll tell them everything. They'll understand. I have no one but you in the world now. And I'm ready to live, however much I have to break and topple and turn upside down. I *will* live. I *will* live. Claire. You haven't heard any news of me for three days now. Three days of anxiety, like the time you had 'flu and I thought you'd let me down. Perhaps you've heard about what happened and you're sad because you think I was involved in it – but I wasn't, I'm here, and thinking of you, Claire. Give me just a little longer.

I have to tell this story. I have to.

One evening before bed, while I was on the dish-washing team, two weeks after I arrived, Lonia came looking for me.

'Come into my office, David, I have something to say to you.'

I immediately thought, as usual, you'd heard news of my parents. And as usual, it was something else.

'You're going to the grammar school in G., starting next week. There's no one here who can help you in your studies. And learning, you see, is a sacred duty. Knowledge is the most precious gift we have, a gift we can pass on to other people. Knowledge is a step taken towards equality, tolerance, love, justice. We must arm ourselves to face life, and I don't mean with pistols and sten guns. Words are just as strong a weapon against those who exploit others.'

I didn't care much about those who exploit others, but I liked the idea of the grammar school. I'd be able to go out, breathe more freely, see the outside world as it really was. And I would learn and learn and learn, for my mother, for my father, so that when we met again they'd see how much progress I'd made.

'Oh, and another thing, David, you're going to Monsieur Legendre for piano lessons twice a week. You really do have musical talent.'

I took Lonia by surprise when I flung my arms round her neck and kissed her. But she was giving me such wonderful presents, exactly like my father and my mother: all these splendid things just for me. Like the bicycle borrowed in the village. I got up very early in the morning to cycle a good ten kilometres of hilly road, up and down, in dew, black ice, mud, rain, weariness. I felt very happy as I entered the dark building of the grammar school next to St Peter's Church. I was intoxicated with freedom. I was even glad to see that sadist the deputy head, who had caught hold of one of the little boys and lifted him off the ground, practically wrenching his ears off in the process. You were a real bastard, sir. You still are. But simply by being there you told me I was like the others, among other boys like myself, normal, subject to punishments, bullying, rewards. Mostly rewards, in fact, even though I was out of breath from the cycle ride at first, with a stitch in my side and my legs like jelly. First in composition. First in just about everything. Top of the class. My revenge. Lonia was pleased, and it was a kind of revenge which didn't upset anyone. The others decided the new boy was bright, and that was that. There was some jealousy, of course, but when I made a few friends, I always had to preserve total silence when I was asked harmless questions.

'Where are you from, then?'

'What do your parents do?'

I turned it off with a joke and a bit of banter.

It was so good to be like the others, laughing at nothing to speak of, and not always serious like

Lonia, who had sent me to that cheerful black grammar school building. The familiar smell of ink, paper, library books covered with brown paper. And the pleasure of scuffling with the others too, over nothing to speak of. It meant I was alive.

But even school was nothing beside my real life. I lived that at Monsieur Legendre's, with the piano, and my fingers on its keyboard twice a week.

'And don't forget to practise, David.'

'Goodbye, Monsieur Legendre.'

He shook hands with me. He shook hands with Claire. And then we were both out on his landing, not daring to speak to each other.

I had never been so keen on the piano and my practising before. They made me think of Claire. I got very absent-minded.

'David, you can always come and see me any time you want a talk.' Lonia thought I was in a grief-stricken state and had caught the sadness the others felt. We were all infected by it in turn. Homesickness. But in fact I was wonderfully happy as I covered up my tracks, telling lies. Thank you for teaching me to tell lies, Lonia.

Claire. The more I write, the more I know I have to write about something horrible, hateful. I want to put it off. So I'm talking to you now, only ten kilometres away, in your handsome big house with its iron gates and its garden. Maybe you're back at Monsieur Legendre's and there's someone else at the white piano instead of me. But don't worry, I'll be coming back very soon. Just let me wait a little longer before everything boils up and explodes and the world loses all meaning – or maybe, once I've finished this story, gets its meaning back.

I fell in love with you the moment I saw you. The very first time. Your long fair hair, your light summer dress, your sweet face, your graceful neck. Your long fingers caressing the keys. And your blush when you saw me.

It was like a book or a film. Love at first sight, real love. I spent my nights thinking of you.

Coming out of school I lagged behind just to try to catch a glimpse of you.

And then there was the first time I walked you home, or rather to the corner of your road, because of your parents. I talked and talked, about anything that came into my head, remember? I told you about this amazing poet I'd been reading, Apollinaire. I didn't have his works, but I'd read his poems in the library. All the time I talked to you there was a single phrase going round in my head, hammering away like a machine gun: 'I love you, I love you, I love you.' I dared not let it out, though. Might I touch you? Both hands were occupied holding my handlebars.

Do you still think about me?

I want to see you, hear you, touch your arms, your hands, your mouth. I love you. I love you. It's only been three days. Three days in which everything turned upside down.

I talked to you about Apollinaire. Next time you

talked to me about Rimbaud. And then, just before we parted, you opened your satchel. Abruptly, you handed me a book and then shot off without turning round. I just heard you saying, 'Don't look at it until you get home.'

Home!

I disobeyed. There was a marker in the page you meant. The book was Apollinaire's collection of poems called *Alcools*. I stopped by the roadside and read it.

### The Farewell

> I have plucked this sprig of heather
> In an autumn season late
> No more shall we be together
> Scent of time sprig of heather
> Remember that I shall wait

The title leapt out at me first. It was all over. This was Claire's way of telling me so. She felt ashamed. She had left me. No one would ever love me. I read it again, to make sure what you wanted to tell me. Then I came to the last line and started crying. I was an idiot, a total, utter idiot. The last line was underlined in fine black pencil. 'Remember that I shall wait.'

How can I describe my happiness? How could I thank her?

How could I show her my love? I cycled twice as fast as usual, shouting as I went along the road, zigzagging wildly. She would wait for me. I felt like turning back at once, but of course I couldn't. Anyway, I was so happy I didn't mind waiting another three days for my next visit to Monsieur Legendre's big room, when I would see her again and return her book.

When Lonia saw me coming back smiling broadly, she thought I was over the worst and my depression had lifted.

'You see, things do work out. You must never be discouraged.'

And she gave me a pleased smile.

Never before had I put so much energy into helping the little ones practise writing their capital letters before supper.

Never before had I had such difficulty getting to sleep after supper.

Claire was braver than me.

In bed, when the story was over, I told myself other stories, stories Lonia could hardly have imagined, and they took my penis to the limits of what it could bear. Love and pain. Love and the wonderful feeling after that explosion friends at school called jerking off. A horrible expression. An expression which didn't in the least suit the thoughts that went with it.

I saw your body naked at that moment, Claire, a wonderful body, and it was for me, just for me. And I gave you everything I had.

It was hopeless trying to sleep. I got up. I went

downstairs to the classroom, borrowing the dormitory candle.

I had brought my school books in case Lonia found me there. I could say I had homework to do. I tore a sheet of paper out of my maths exercise book and wrote the most beautiful words of love I could think of. I wrote that I loved you too. I wrote about your hair, your smile, how good I felt with you beside me even if you didn't say a word. I picked up your book again. After a final 'I love you', I added a PS, a line of poetry: 'My eyes are slowly poisoning themselves for yours.'

You've no idea how much more I felt like adding! But by now I was lightheaded with love and weariness. I folded the letter, hid it in the book, went to bed and fell asleep, and who cared about the marks my boundless love had left on the sheets?

Then I had to wait before I could give you my letter, feeling tempted to tear it up because it was too silly, too shocking, too – well, too everything. I had to wait for your first glance as I went into Monsieur Legendre's room. I saw you understood. And then the lies. We gained time by saying Monsieur Legendre wanted us to give a recital. Lonia accepted everything I told her. How could a child who had been in her charge tell lies? Unthinkable. Our long walks. Your look of surprise when you heard I was Jewish. My smile, which I hid, when you said you'd pray for me at Mass. I didn't tell you anything about my past troubles, of course. They *were* past. I was with you.

That was enough. We would never, never part again. Our first kiss, in the wood, after telling more lies. Your body against mine. Your warmth. Your modesty. My own, and then our immodesty. Our love.

Come back, come back, I'm waiting for you. I want you with me. You're the only person in the world who might make me able to smile again.

I thought of you the whole time: in school, in the town, at 'home', during the rehearsals for the Fourteenth of July concert, which began well in advance. I had nothing to do but play the piano accompaniment to the *Marseillaise* while the others sang. Lonia went to a lot of trouble to explain things to us. All about Liberty, Equality and Fraternity. Maurice and Hanna were to take the parts of Louis XVI and Marie-Antoinette. However, Maurice refused to play the part of a tyrant who exploited his people. Sonia couldn't seem to learn her bit of the Declaration of the Rights of Man, which was to be recited in spoken chorus. Lonia went from one to the other. Samuel was the only really happy person; he was pleased to be playing the part of Robespierre and crushing the despots.

Robespierre. The name of my Underground station. Closed now. But I could get out at the Porte de Montreuil or at the Croix de Chavaux, and go home on foot. I hated Samuel. Nobody understood why I began sniffing when Lonia told us all about Robespierre, known as the Incorruptible. He wanted a better world where all men would be equal, as they were in the Soviet Union. Nobody there knew that Robespierre was also the name of a station on my line. The familiar names of the stations. Mairie de Montreuil. Croix de Chavaux. Robespierre. Porte de Montreuil. Maraîchers. Buzenval. Nation. Mother. Father.

Lonia had no time to bother about me. She kept on about the aristocrats, the peasants dying of starvation, great lords, injustice, slavery, the taking of the Bastille.

I promise you, Claire, only Robespierre could have made me forget you just for an instant. Forgive me; it was just too much.

And then the next day it was all forgotten, because I saw you again.

You had good news. Everyone was saying that the Germans were retreating, there were more and more trains being derailed, the end was near. You were happy for me. And sad too, because that might mean I'd be leaving, going home, back to my family. I saw your eyes go misty.

It was only three days ago, remember? And remember the crazy plan we'd made because we couldn't bear to part?

'It's easy − I'll tell Lonia I had to stay in after school, and then it was too late to cycle back, so Monsieur Legendre let me stay the night. That should do the trick. What about your parents?'

You shrugged your shoulders.

So we met in the woods after school. You'd

brought warm blankets, and we spent the night lying side by side. You said, 'No, I can't.' I understood. You caressed me, I caressed you, and we fell asleep lying on the moss.

Early in the morning I kissed you on the lips and then mounted my bicycle.

'See you tomorrow, Claire. I love you.'

'I love you too. See you tomorrow.'

There wasn't any tomorrow. I'm here, and I must finish this fast, fast, even if I leave out some of the details. But I must finish it without lying or cheating. Because only then can there possibly be any tomorrow. Just now I don't have the strength to imagine it.

It was hardly daylight. I had nothing to regret. I had done what your sadness and my desire made me do. Too bad if Lonia didn't believe me. Too bad if I'd betrayed her trust. I was exhausted. I felt proud. I could face the whole world. Nothing was beyond me now.

I went over my lie to make sure it sounded all right. I mustn't give myself away. Mustn't give *you* away. I pedalled quietly along. It had been a wonderful night. For a moment I felt dizzy. I was all right, though. I went on again, towards the rising sun.

And then, unexpectedly, as I came to the crossroads and was about to leave the road and go up the lane, there was Monsieur Rigal in front of me. I braked abruptly. He caught up with me in time.

'Don't go up there, David lad, don't go up there. They're in the house. In the house. Come with me.'

I had no idea what he meant.

Of course I was going up there. What did I have to fear? Who were at the house? What did he mean? Well, I'd soon see. Monsieur Rigal couldn't stop me. He had to follow me at a run. I didn't go up the lane though. I left my bicycle behind and plunged into the undergrowth. He tried to stop me, calling hoarsely, 'Don't go, don't go. Please don't!'

I was not afraid. I did not feel frightened. But when I came within sight of the house I dropped to the ground, with Monsieur Rigal close beside me.

There was a lorry with a tarpaulin over it in front of the stone steps, and an armoured car, and two motorbikes. A man in black SS uniform and cap was shouting orders I didn't understand.

My legs are shaking as I write. They came out, one by one. All of them. Lonia, Maurice, Hanna, the twins, little Perla, Ida, Rachel, Samuel, Hélène. They had hardly had time to dress. One by one: my brothers, my sisters, my friends, my dear ones. As soon as they reached the last step two German soldiers picked them up and threw them into the lorry. I started getting to my feet. Monsieur Rigal forced me down to the ground, putting his large hand over my mouth to silence me. Then, last of all, I saw Lonia come out. She pushed the two soldiers aside and climbed into the lorry by herself. The engine was running. The motorbikes went first, then the lorry, then the armoured car and a black front-wheel drive car with the man in black inside it.

They passed fifty metres from us. In the cold early morning air, the sound of the *Marseillaise* being sung in every accent in Europe rose from the tarpaulin-covered lorry. I recognized Lonia's voice, stronger than all the others. They were all in the lorry, under the tarpaulin. All except one, who was running desperately, too fast for Monsieur Rigal to catch him, not knowing where he was going.

One who was howling silently inside, one who abandoned you. One who betrayed you. One who didn't go all the way to the very end with you. A coward.

Goodbye. Perhaps it's not all over, perhaps all isn't lost yet. Please say you don't hold it against me. Tell me I'm with you. Tell me it was only Monsieur Rigal who stopped me. I ought to have been with you. That was my place. I am with you wherever you go.

I've written it all now. The house is empty. Father, Mother, Lonia, I didn't do it on purpose. I swear I didn't. I've finished. I have nothing else to add. Who cares if my tears fall on the paper and wash the words away? I've told the truth, the whole truth. I would like to have been singing the *Marseillaise* too. But I was prevented.

I'm fifteen years old. Fifteen short years of life. Now what?

From the window I can see Monsieur Rigal approaching with his heavy tread, bringing me something to eat. I'm not hungry.

Lonia, why didn't you make them wait for me, so that I could go with you all? You knew I wasn't there at roll call. You had no right to abandon me, leaving me alone in this empty house.

Claire.